Enjoy!
love
Susan Davies
x

Dedication

Dedicated to my three little inspirations,
my Grandchildren Alfie, Harry and Evie.
Also my children Kirsty, Hayley and Ashley.
Love you all to the moon and back. XXX
Nanna Yia for all your magical stories and
instilling in me my love for books.
To all the wonderful children I've taught at
Cadoxton School. You will always hold a
special place in my heart.

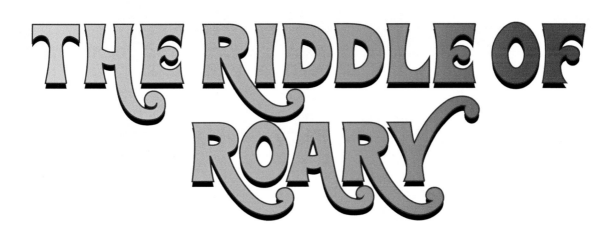

THE RIDDLE OF ROARY

Written by: Susan Davies
Illustrations by: Kiran Rana

ALFIE GEORGE STEEN had
only one dream:
to work in a zoo and be
part of a team.

He wished and wished that his dream would come true.
Then one day, the call came and they said... WE... WANT... YOU!

Well, the problem with Alfie was,
he **disliked** going to bed.
He'd stay up through the night
watching TV instead.

He looked after the lions, but that morning he was late. He hadn't slept and was tired and...

Left open the gate... A lion called Roary
ran out like a shot
and was hiding from Alfie who
felt such a clot.

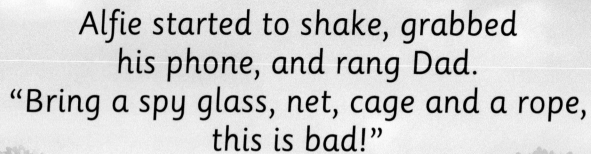

Alfie started to shake, grabbed
his phone, and rang Dad.
"Bring a spy glass, net, cage and a rope,
this is bad!"

EXIT ZOO

So off they both went looking
for a lion to trap,
searched in parks, under benches,
and followed a map.

They entered a forest, right next to a lane.
Alfie looked through his spy glass,
"I've spotted a mane!"
They crept up so slowly, not taking a chance.
Then threw out the net.
Whoosh! And started to dance.

8

"We've got him." said Dad.
"I really am sure.
Now pull back the net,
wrestle him to the floor."

Uh-oh, they weren't right.
Oh no! They were wrong.
In the net was no lion but...
wig-wearing Miss Tong.

"**My hair!**" screamed Miss Tong.
"Oh no," said Dad. They'd trapped a bald
lady who was ever so mad.
So quickly, they freed her and ran
as fast as they could,
to the top of the hill and into the woods.

11

Alfie looked through his spy glass,
"I've spotted his tail!
Get the rope to lasso and
let's follow his trail."
Whoosh!

"We've got him." said Dad.
"I really am sure.
Now pull back the rope,
wrestle him to the floor."

Uh-oh, they weren't right.
Oh no! They were wrong.
In the rope was no lion but a... snake
six feet long.

"**Hiss!**" said the snake. "Oh no," said Dad.
"Let go of me now before I get mad!"
Alfie undid the rope and let the snake go.
Then he looked through his spy glass and
searched high and low.

"I've spotted him Dad. His teeth I can see.
He's hiding right there. He's under that tree."
They pulled out the rope, got it ready to tie,
laying still on their bellies, not making a sigh
Whoosh!

"We've got him." said Dad.
"I really am sure.
Now pull back the rope,
wrestle him to the floor."

Uh-oh, they weren't right.
Oh no! They were wrong.
In the rope was no lion but a... fox,
lean and long.

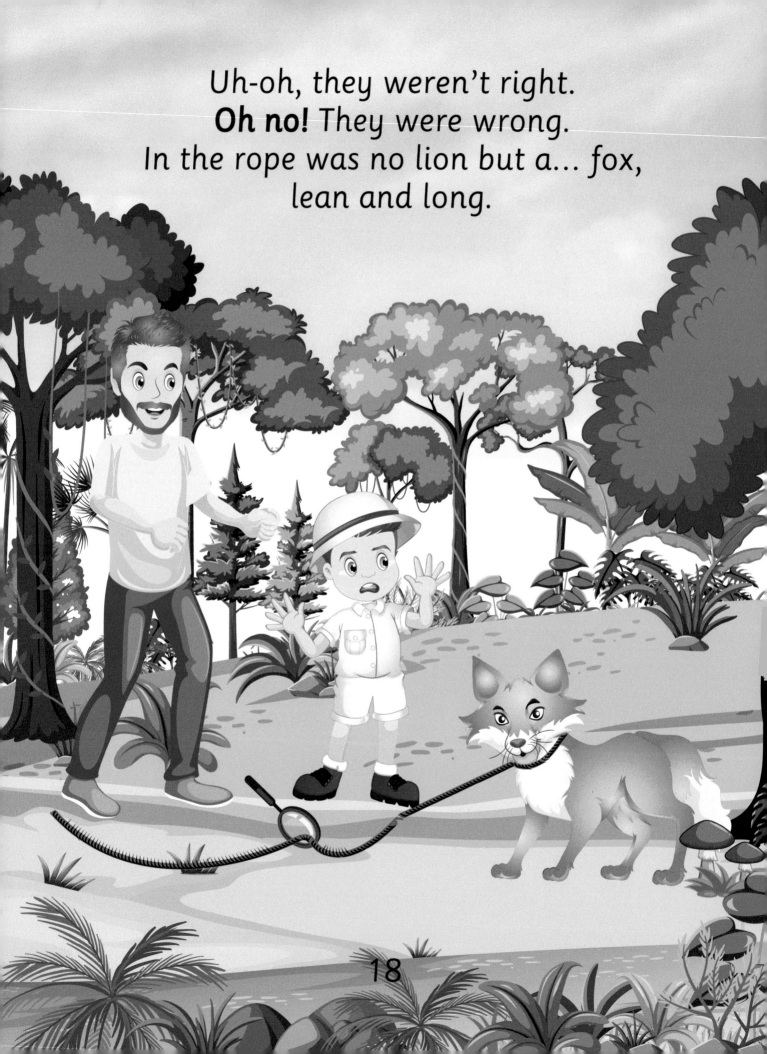

"Grrr!" said the fox.
"Oh no," said Dad.
"Let go of me now, before I get mad!"
Alfie undid the rope and the fox ran away.
Then he picked up his spy glass to see
fields full of hay.

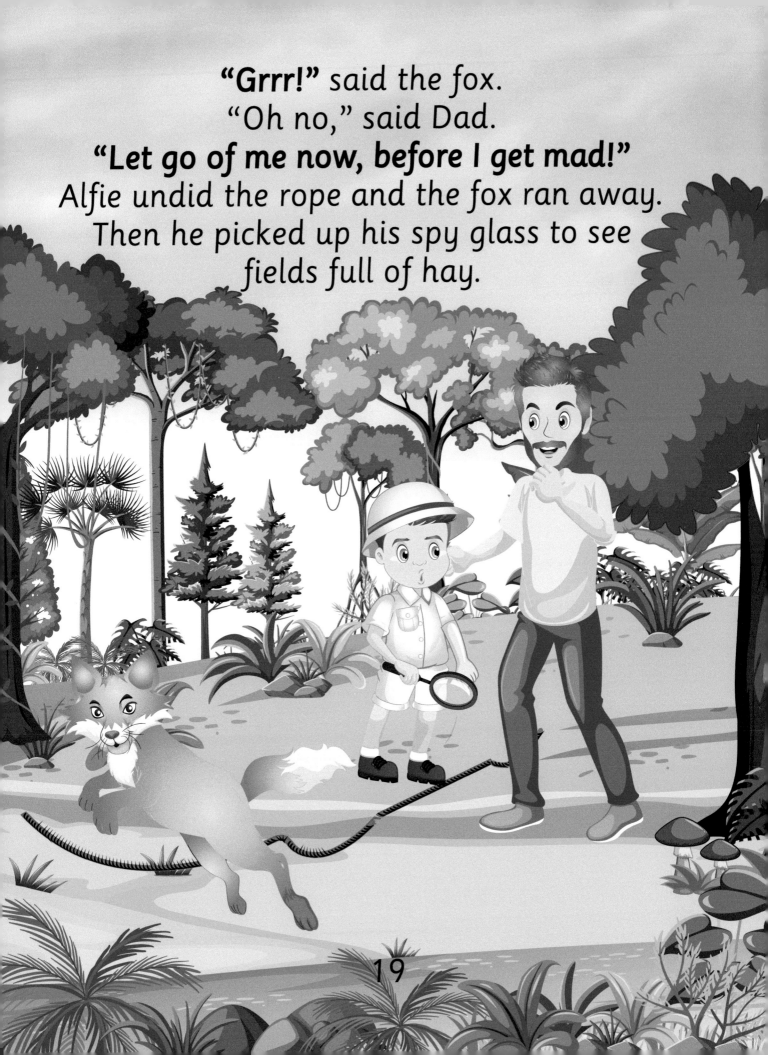

"I've spotted him Dad.
With his razor-sharp claws,
take care, we don't want to end up in his jaws.
He's over that hill to the left of the lake.
Now get the cage ready, this lion we'll take."
Whoosh!

"We've got him." said Dad.
"This time, I am sure.
Now pull back the cage,
wrestle him to the floor."

Uh-oh, they weren't right.
Oh no! They were wrong.
In the cage was no lion but a... croc,
green and strong.

"**Snap!**" went the croc. "Oh no," said Dad.
"**Let go of me now before I get mad!**"
They released him quickly
and climbed up a tree.
Then stared in the distance
to look for Roary.

23

"It's no use. Let's give up.
He'll never be found.
We've looked everywhere and
explored every sound."

(MUCH LATER)
Well, Roary was smart and he'd
put on a disguise.
Then he boarded a plane,
and took to the skies.

The last Alfie heard, when telling his story;
The lion was back in the jungle and his
new name was...
KING ROARY!